SNOW GHOST

By Robin Wasserman
Illustrated by Duendes del Sur

Hello Reader — Level 1

No part of this work may be reproduced in whole or in part, or stored in a retrieval system, or transmitted in any form or by any means, electronic, mechanical, photocopying, recording, or otherwise, without written permission of the publisher. For information regarding permission, write to Scholastic Inc., Attention: Permissions Department, 555 Broadway, New York, NY 10012.

ISBN 0-439-31845-9

12 11 10 9 8 7 6 5 4   2 3 4 5 6/0

Designed by Maria Stasavage
Printed in the U.S.A.
First Scholastic printing, November 2001

SCHOLASTIC INC.

New York   Toronto   London   Auckland   Sydney
Mexico City   New Delhi   Hong Kong   Buenos Aires

and the gang were on a .

They were building a .

 made out of 🍪 🍪.

 made a out of a 🥕.

 made a 👄 out of .

made arms out of .

put his 🧢 and 🧣 on top of the ⛄ .

"Like, this is the best ⛄ ever!" said .

Then  , , and went

down the on their .
and slid on a .

When they went back to their

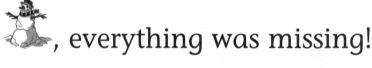 , everything was missing!

The 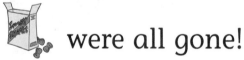 and the and the

were all gone!

"Did a  take them?" asked
.

"A  !"  shouted.

He dug a hole in the 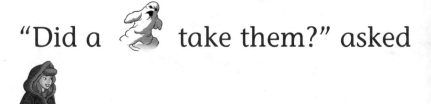.

Then he jumped in.

"Come out,

need to look for clues."

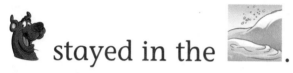 stayed in the.

"Come out, ," said . "We

need to find our missing things."

stayed in the 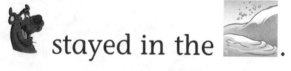.

"Come out, ," said ,

"and I'll give you some ."

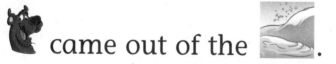 came out of the.

"There are no 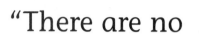," said .

"Like, maybe the flew away from the ," said .

"Jinkies!" said . "I found our ."

She pointed up.

The was hanging from a .

looked for clues.

He found a .

He ran toward it.

He slipped.

He fell.

 rolled and rolled and rolled.

rolled halfway down the

.

When he stopped, he heard

strange noises.

"A !" shouted.

He dug a hole in the .

Then he jumped in.

The gang came down to find

him.

"Come out, ," said .

"You solved the mystery."

 poked his head out of the

 .

He saw the ●● and the 🎩 and

the 🥕.

He saw the 📦.

Then he saw what had

taken them.

It was not a 🐰.

It was a 🐦!

"What about our ?" asked .

"I have an idea," said .

The gang worked hard.

When they were done, said,

"Zoinks! Our looks just like

a real !"

"A !" shouted.

He dug a hole in the .

Then he jumped in.

Did you spot all the picture clues in this Scooby-Doo mystery?

Each picture clue is on a flash card. Ask a grown-up to cut out the flash cards. Then try reading the words on the back of the cards. The pictures will be your clue.

Reading is fun with Scooby-Doo!